HOW TO LOOK AFTER YOUR
DINOSAUR

FRAGILE
HANDLE WITH CARE

First published 2017 by Nosy Crow Ltd
14 Baden Place, Crosby Row,
London SE1 1YW
www.nosycrow.com

ISBN 978 0 85763 928 8 (HB)
ISBN 978 0 85763 929 5 (PB)

Nosy Crow and associated logos are trademarks
and/or registered trademarks of Nosy Crow Ltd

Text and illustrations © Jason Cockcroft 2017
The right of Jason Cockcroft to be identified as the author and illustrator
of this work has been asserted.

A CIP catalogue record for this book is available from the British Library.

Papers used by Nosy Crow are made from wood grown in
sustainable forests.

Printed and bound in Turkey by Imago

1 2 3 4 5 6 7 8 9 (HB)
 2 3 4 5 6 7 8 9 (PB)

FRAGILE
HANDLE WITH CARE

POST

DEC

HOW TO LOOK AFTER YOUR
DINOSAUR

nosy crow

Congratulations on your new pet!

When you first meet him,
you might find that he is
surprisingly shy.

But don't worry . . .

. . . he'll **SOON** come out of his shell!

It's **really** important to make your dinosaur feel at home, so why not start with a healthy **breakfast** to give him plenty of **energy** for the day ahead?

Don't worry if your dinosaur is slow to try new foods . . .

. . . he'll **quickly**
find his appetite.

After breakfast, your dinosaur may get **fidgety**. This is a **perfect** time to go for a **gentle** walk in the park.

However, it won't be long until your pet needs to poo, so it's advisable to carry a bucket and spade **at all times.**

Sometimes, a bucket and spade . . .

. . . will not be enough.

Most dinosaurs can't swim, and your pet
may be **frightened** near water.

It's best to avoid playing
near beaches, lakes or rivers.

A small pond or puddle can be great **fun**, though . . . as long as your dinosaur is **properly** dressed.

Dinosaurs **love** company.
Why not encourage your pet
to meet new people and
make friends?

After all, no one knows better
than a dinosaur that friendship
is all about . . .

. . . sharing.

Remember to feed your dinosaur **regularly**.
Dinner can be a **very** excitable time,
but if you're quiet and calm . . .

. . . he might just
settle down.

After a full day at
the park, your dinosaur
will be feeling tired.

So try to get him home at
a **reasonable** hour.

Once you are home, don't forget
that **all** dinosaurs thrive on a
proper bedtime **routine.**

After a light supper, a bath
is a **good** idea.

Make sure that the water is not too hot, and always use an **appropriate** amount of soap.

When your dinosaur is squeaky clean,
consider sharing a **bedtime** story.

Try not to choose books that are **too exciting,**
as these will keep your pet awake.

Your dinosaur's story time is a moment for **calm** and **quiet**.

And, always **remember,**
if you treat him well,
your dinosaur can be . . .

. . . a friend for life.

WEEK
NLY!
FOR 1
SALE
JY ONE
ET ONE
FREE!
DINO EGG
COMPANY
FOR ALL
YOUR DINO
NEEDS!